Word Wise with Wordsworth

Word Advantage™

a diamond in the rough—someone or something with hidden potential (idiom, page 21)

autograph—someone's name written in their own handwriting (noun, page 7)

concealed—hidden or covered (adjective, page 16)

courage—bravery (noun, page 24)

ferocious—vicious or cruel (adjective, page 15)

inspire—to encourage or influence (verb, page 8)

landmark—something that helps people identify a location (noun, page 28)

launch—to send off or propel (verb, page 18, *launched*)

linger—to hang around, wait, or delay (verb, page 22, *lingered*)

nimble—quick-moving or agile (adjective, page 15)

opportunity—a good chance or moment to do something (noun, page 13)

perceptive—aware or observant (adjective, page 10)

potential—an ability that is possible but doesn't exist yet (noun, page 21)

precious—very valuable or costly (adjective, page 7)

resume—to begin again (verb, page 13, *resumed*)

scan—to read or look over quickly (verb, page 29, *scanned*)

scowl—to frown or glare (verb, 11, *scowled*)

snout—a nose, usually an animal's (noun, page 17)

stellar—outstanding (adjective, page 24)

vanish—to disappear suddenly (verb, page 26)

wary—cautious or suspicious (adjective, page 18)

Cover design by Mark A. Neston Design

Published by Scholastic Inc., 90 Old Sherman Turnpike, Danbury, CT 06816.

ISBN 0-7172-8688-6

Printed in the U.S.A.

First Printing, February 2007

A DIAMOND IN THE ROUGH

by Quinn Alexander
Illustrated by Kelly Kennedy

SCHOLASTIC INC.

New York Toronto London Auckland Sydney
Mexico City New Delhi Hong Kong Buenos Aires

Wordsworth, the class pet, must have heard the sound first, because he squawked loudly and started hopping around his cage. Then Abby, Marco, and Mrs. Harris heard it, too. Someone was singing in the hallway. "Take me out to the ball game. Take me out with the crowd . . ." A moment later Mr. Keys, the Webster School custodian, came into the room.

"Hello, Mrs. Harris. Hi, kids," he said. "I've got something to show you." He held up a tattered old baseball, as if it were a **precious** gem. "This was passed down by my great-grandfather Theodore Alexander. It was signed by the first kids who played in the ball field at Cloverhill Park."

He handed the baseball to Marco, who rolled it around in his fingers. The worn surface was covered with faded **autographs**. One name stood out among the others: *Buster Blaze.*

"This is so cool!" said Marco. "We've been looking up stuff about Buster Blaze Field for our history project."

Mr. Keys nodded. "Mrs. Harris told me. That's why I brought in the ball."

Marco and Abby had been digging through history books after school to learn what their town was like a hundred years ago. They knew that the baseball diamond at Cloverhill Park was named Buster Blaze Field, but they hadn't been able to find out who Buster Blaze was.

"So do *you* know who Buster Blaze was?" Abby asked Mr. Keys.

"It's been a mystery for as long as I can remember," he replied. He turned to go. "When you're done looking at the ball, just leave it on Mrs. Harris's desk. I'll pick it up later."

"Thanks, Mr. Keys," said the kids.

"I'm glad you brought it in," added Mrs. Harris. "I'm sure it will **inspire** the children."

The custodian strolled out of the room, singing again. Then Mrs. Harris left, too, heading for the school office to make some photocopies.

"Open the door! Open the door!" Wordsworth squawked the moment she left.

Marco and Abby knew what those words meant: Adventure was just around the corner!

Abby flung open the cage door, and Wordsworth flew out of the room and down the hall. Mr. Keys was walking into another classroom, so he didn't see Wordsworth zoom by, with the kids hot on his tail. The bird headed straight for the back of the custodian's room. It seemed he would crash right into the supply shelves. But at the last second, the wall melted away, forming a dark, mysterious tunnel.

Marco and Abby followed Wordsworth through the tunnel. As before, there was a loud pop and a burst of white light; and they found themselves standing near a field in the Cloverhill of one hundred years ago.

Abby stared at her clothes. In earlier trips to the past, her jeans and hoodie had been transformed into dresses worn by girls in the early 1900s. This time, she was wearing the same sort of old-fashioned pants that Marco was wearing, and her long hair was tucked under a cap.

"Hey! This is weird," she said. "Why am I wearing pants? And what's with the hat?"

"Maybe it's a different kind of disguise," suggested Marco.

"Very **perceptive**," said Wordsworth. "As you may have observed on previous visits, girls in this time period don't wear pants."

"Then why—," began Abby, but she was cut off by the crack of a wooden bat hitting a baseball, followed by the sound of kids cheering.

Wordsworth fluttered onto Marco's shoulder, and he and Abby stepped out onto the field. A bunch of boys were playing baseball on a weedy field nearby.

"I *love* baseball!" Abby exclaimed. "Let's see if we can play, too."

"Ahem," said Wordsworth. "I regret to say that girls in this time period don't play baseball."

Abby **scowled**. "Why not? I'm a good player. Just ask Marco."

But Marco was staring off into the distance. "You know," he said slowly, "I think this is where Cloverhill Park is today."

"You might be right," said Wordsworth. "I'll give it a bird's-eye view." And with that, he took off.

One of the older boys jogged over. He was tall and seemed strong, and he had a welcoming smile. "Hello, my name's Ted," he said. "Do you two want to play?"

"Sure," said Marco. "My name's Marco, and this is—"

"Jimmy," Abby said quickly.

For a moment Marco was confused. Why had Abby introduced herself as Jimmy? That was her brother's name. But then he figured it out. Abby was afraid that if the kids knew she was a girl, they wouldn't let her play.

Ted looked the two of them up and down. "You—," he pointed to Abby, "you'll be in right field. And you—," he pointed to Marco, "you'll be on the team that's up to bat."

Marco and Abby took their places, and the game **resumed**. The sun was shining, there was a cool breeze, and the air smelled of clover. It was a perfect day for baseball, and Marco was having a great time. But Abby was not so happy. She realized that Ted had seen her as a skinny little kid. So he had stuck her in right field, where she couldn't do much harm.

Abby looked for an **opportunity** to impress the other players. It came in the third inning, when Ted cracked a thundering home run over a fence beyond left field.

"The ball landed in Mr. Bradford's yard," shouted the left fielder. "*I'm* not getting it."

"Me, either," yelled the shortstop. "I'm not crazy."

Abby figured she could prove herself by retrieving the ball. "No big deal. I'll get it," she said. She sprinted across the outfield, showing off her speed. Then, in a **nimble** move, she grabbed the top of the wooden fence and leaped over to the other side.

As she did, she heard Ted call, "Jimmy! Watch out for the dog!"

The dog? Abby's heart sank.

Abby landed in a crouching position. She looked left and right. A garden took up most of the backyard. Beyond it was a small, well-kept house. There was no sign of a **ferocious** dog—but no sign of the baseball, either.

As she tiptoed forward, Abby heard a thump from behind. She whirled around, expecting to see the open jaws of a dog the size of a horse. But it was just Marco, jumping the fence.

"Didn't you hear what they said?" whispered Marco. "There's a dog in this yard."

"Maybe it's napping," Abby whispered back. "I might as well grab the ball while I'm here."

Easier said than done. The ball wasn't on the lawn, which was as trim as an infield. So Abby checked out the garden, slipping between two rows of young corn.

"Come on, let's go," Marco said anxiously.

Abby stopped. She peered down a row of strawberry plants. There, **concealed** beneath one of the plants, like a large egg under a small hen, was the baseball. As she reached out to grab it, something flashed in the corner of her eye—something moving very fast.

Dog alert!

The dog bounding their way looked big enough to use a baseball bat as a toothpick.

Marco took off. "Run!" he shouted.

Abby snatched the ball and ran after him. But there was no way they were going to reach the fence in time. In fact, the dog would have been on them in a second if a large white bird hadn't suddenly appeared from nowhere. Like a dive-bomber, Wordsworth zoomed past the dog's **snout**, drawing its attention away from Marco and Abby.

"Head for the tree!" Wordsworth called.

An apple tree stood near the back fence. It had low-hanging branches, just within reach.

Jamming the baseball into her pocket, Abby **launched** herself at a branch on one side of the tree. Marco took aim at the other side. As they swung up into the branches, they expected the dog to clamp onto their legs. But Wordsworth made another daring pass by the dog's powerful mouth, which gave Abby and Marco just enough time to pull their feet out of reach.

"Now what do we do?" Marco said, panting.

"I don't know, but it looks like we've got company," said Abby. A man was making his way slowly across the yard.

"Easy, Tiny, easy," said the man. He took a hold of the dog's collar and stared up into the tree. "My, my," he said. "I thought this tree only grew apples. But I seem to have a nice crop of children this year." He laughed at his own joke and then introduced himself as Mr. Bradford. "Why don't you two *drop* in for a visit?" he added.

Marco gave the dog a **wary** look. "Are you sure it's safe?" he asked, as he and Abby climbed down from the tree.

"I'm sure," said Mr. Bradford. "Tiny might drown you in slobber, but he won't bite."

"We're sorry about getting into your garden," said Abby. "We were looking for this." She held up the baseball as proof.

"That's all right," said Mr. Bradford. "I give you credit. You're the first kids brave enough to come into my yard." He looked at the fence, where the other players were now standing. "Maybe your friends would like to join us. I've got a big bowl of strawberries that will go to waste unless I have help eating them."

Mr. Bradford opened his front gate. The boys eyed the dog nervously as they trooped into the yard. But Tiny had settled down on the porch and was taking a nap—and drooling.

"I've watched you children play baseball many an afternoon," Mr. Bradford said. "You look a little rough around the edges, but you're good players. You have **potential**. In fact, you're a lot like that baseball field."

"We are?" asked Ted.

Mr. Bradford nodded. "That field is **a diamond in the rough**. It has lots of weeds now, but it could be a beautiful baseball field someday."

"I believe it," said Abby.

"That's the spirit! You can't judge things by the way they look at first glance," said Mr. Bradford, staring at Abby. "And what's your name?"

"Jimmy," said Abby.

"Well, then—*Jimmy*," said Mr. Bradford, "how about if you and your friend help me bring the refreshments out to the porch?"

Marco followed Mr. Bradford inside. Abby trailed behind more slowly. It seemed as if Mr. Bradford knew her secret. The question was: would he tell the kids? As she **lingered** in the living room, Abby noticed some photos on the wall. Several of them showed Mr. Bradford when he was young. He was wearing a baseball uniform and held a bat over his shoulder, like Paul Bunyan with his ax.

"Wow," said Abby. "You were on a team?"

"That's right. I played in the minor leagues," Mr. Bradford said proudly. "My real name is Blaze Bradford. But back then, they called me Buster Blaze—because I once busted the cover clean off a baseball."

Marco and Abby stared at Mr. Bradford.

"*You're* Buster Blaze?" Abby gasped. She had thought Buster Blaze was a kid, because his name was on Mr. Keys's baseball.

"You've heard of me?" asked Mr. Bradford. "But I haven't played for a long time."

"Believe me. You're really famous, where we come from," said Marco.

Mr. Bradford smiled. "I'm glad to hear that," he said. "I had some **stellar** years. I hit a lot of home runs and stole a lot of bases. But I had to quit when the team owners decided only whites could play in the pro league."

"That isn't fair!" Abby said hotly. "Anybody should be able to play. Girls, too!"

"You've got that right, Jimmy," said Mr. Bradford, and he gave Abby a quick wink.

Abby grinned. She knew her secret was safe with Mr. Bradford.

She and Marco carried the strawberries, a pitcher of ice-cold water, and some glasses out to the porch. For the next half hour, Mr. Bradford spun tales about his baseball days while the kids polished off the berries. As they finished up, Abby handed the baseball to Ted.

"Thanks," said Ted. "This old ball is pretty worn. In fact, the stitching broke, and I had to sew it up. But it's the only one we have, so I'm glad you got it back. That took **courage**, kid." He gave Abby a friendly nudge that nearly knocked her over. Then he turned to Mr. Bradford. "Any chance you would come back to the field with us and show us a few things?" he asked.

"I would love to," said Mr. Bradford.

They all went out to the baseball diamond. Mr. Bradford set them up for batting practice; and when it was her turn, Abby smacked a grounder past the shortstop.

"Good hit, Jimmy," called Mr. Bradford.

At that moment a large white bird swooped low over the outfield. Moving at the speed of a fastball, it **vanished** behind Mr. Bradford's house.

"Hey! What kind of bird was that?" exclaimed one of the kids.

Marco and Abby exchanged a glance. It was Wordsworth, signaling them that it was time to leave. As they slipped away unnoticed, the last thing they saw was Mr. Bradford showing the kids how to throw a curveball.

They found Wordsworth perched on the top of Mr. Bradford's back fence.

"Wordsworth! We got to meet Buster Blaze," said Abby. "He played in the minors, and he's really nice, and he's teaching the kids all sorts of cool stuff."

"I bet he ends up playing ball with them a lot," said Marco. "And that's how the field was named for him."

Wordsworth bobbed his head. "As I've said before, Marco, you and Abby are smart kids. You figured it out. And now it's time to open the door." He pointed to the fence, drawing their attention to a gate they hadn't noticed before. Marco and Abby joined hands and passed through the opening.

With a pop and a flash of light, the three of them were back at school. The kids didn't see Mr. Keys as they headed out of his room, but they heard him singing nearby.

They returned Wordsworth to his cage in the classroom. Then Marco dashed to his desk, where he stored the mysterious old map of Cloverhill. As he unfolded it, a grin spread across his face. A new **landmark** had appeared on the map: a baseball diamond labeled *Buster Blaze Field.*

"Well, *that* took longer than I thought," said Mrs. Harris, hustling into the room a moment later. "I couldn't find some papers I needed. But they were right in front of my nose all along. Sometimes you just need to look—*really look.*"

Abby picked up Mr. Keys's baseball and turned it over in her hands. In one spot, the stitching had been repaired. Could this be the same ball she had returned to Ted? She **scanned** the signatures. There was no *Ted,* but she found *Theodore Alexander.* Suddenly she understood. Ted was Theodore's nickname. She and Marco had played baseball with Mr. Keys's great-grandfather! Quickly she showed Marco what she had discovered.

Marco grinned. "Sometimes you just need to look—*really look,*" he said.

Wordsworth ruffled his crest feathers. "Good work!" the bird squawked.

Get Your Word's Worth

After you finish reading this book together, use the prompts below to spark thoughtful conversation and lively interaction with your child.

♣ A **landmark** helps people know their location while they are following directions. Provide directions from our house to your school using at least two landmarks.

♣ Each person's **autograph** is different from the next. Show me your autograph, and then I'll show you mine.

♣ Abby found the right **opportunity** to prove that she was a team player when the ball landed over the fence. Tell me about a time when you had an opportunity to do something. What did it show people about you?

♣ The baseball was **concealed** below some plants. Look around this room and find three things that are concealed. Give me clues so I can try to guess them.